Moli bin git stak

About the Indigenous Literacy Foundation

The Indigenous Literacy Foundation (ILF) is a national charity working with Aboriginal and Torres Strait Islander remote Communities across Australia. We are Community-led, responding to requests from remote Communities for culturally relevant books, including early learning board books, resources, and programs to support Communities to create and publish their stories in languages of their choice.

First published in 2023 by the Indigenous Literacy Foundation
PO Box H328
Australia Square NSW 1215
ilf.org.au

Cataloging-in-Publication details are available from the National Library of Australia
www.trove.nla.gov.au

ISBN 9781922592583

Typesetting and design by Hazel Lam
Printed by 1010 Printing International Limited, China

Moli bin git stak

Molly gets stuck

Karen Manbulloo bin raidim dijan stori
Julie Haysom, Denise Angelo, Cindy Manfong
and Karen Manbulloo bin drowim ola pitja

Dijan iya Moli.

This is Molly.

Im brabli bigiswan bigibigi.

She's a really big pig.

Im laigim ledan la sheid.

She likes lying in the shade.

Weya im lilbit wetwan en kolwan.

Where it's a bit damp and cool.

Wan dei Moli bin gowin anda det ka.

One day she squeezed under the car.

Im gada sheid deya.

It's shady there.

Bat imin git stak, bobala.

But she got stuck, poor thing.

Im kaan kamat brom deya.

She couldn't come out again.

Wal, im femili dei bin ol trai kolim im...

Her family tried calling her...

Dei bin trai pushum im en pulum im, bat najing.

They tried pushing her and pulling her, but it didn't help.

Dei bin go gedim shabul.

They went and got a shovel.

Bla digimat brom deya.

To dig her out.

Dei bin digim...

They dug...

Dei bin digim...

They dug...

En dei bin digim...

And they dug...

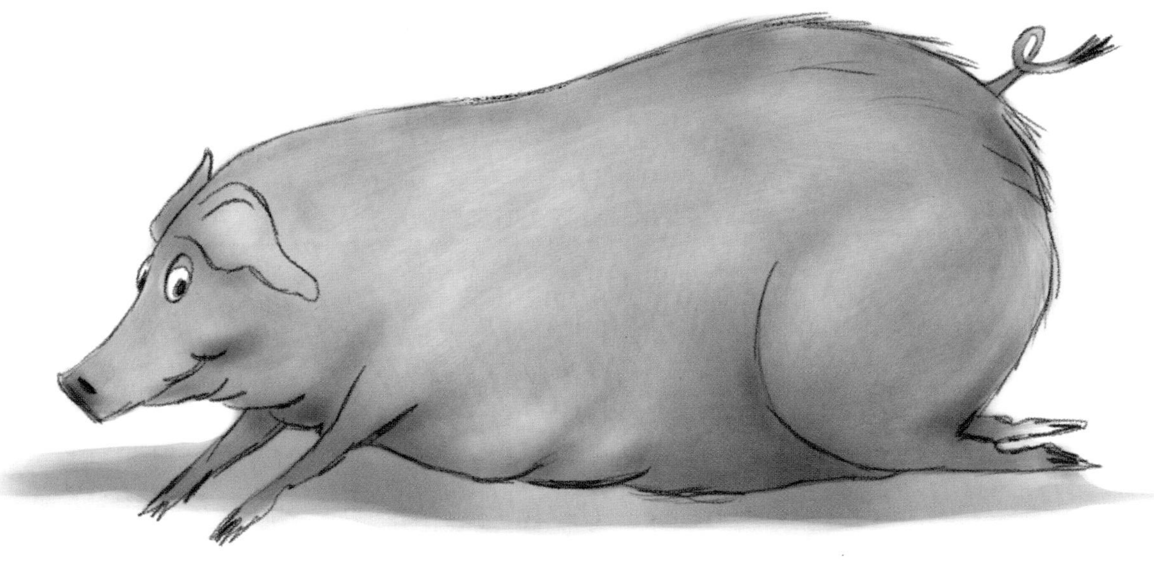

Moli imin git fri!

Molly got free!

Dei bin gibit im woda ba dringkim.

They gave her some water to drink.

Moli neba gowin anda det ka igin.

Molly never goes under that car anymore.

Im go ledan la sheid la tri na.

She goes and lays down in the shade of a tree instead.